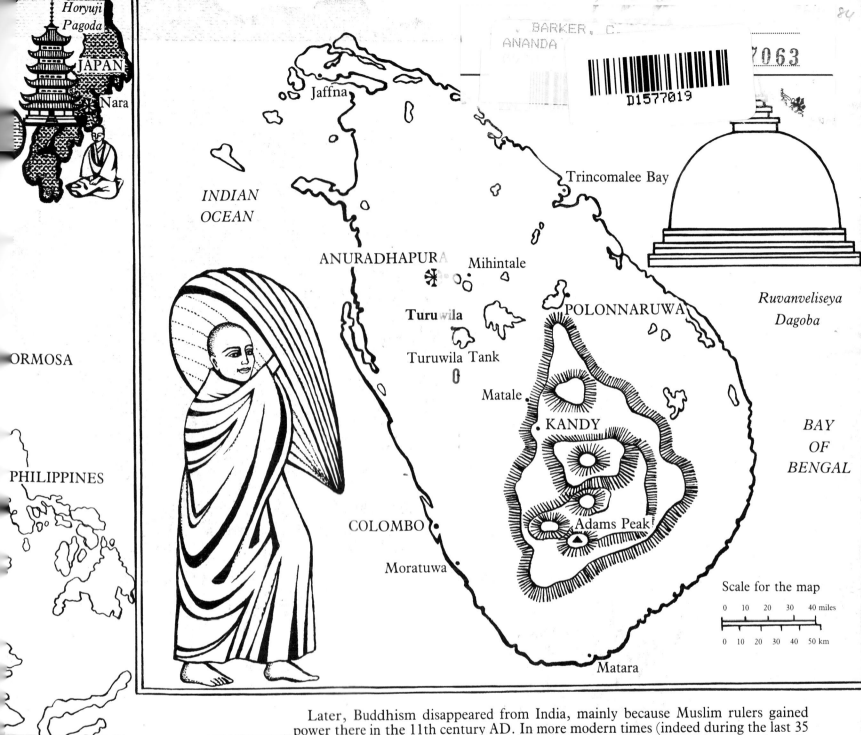

Later, Buddhism disappeared from India, mainly because Muslim rulers gained power there in the 11th century AD. In more modern times (indeed during the last 35 to 40 years), the spread of Communism has meant that Buddhism has virtually disappeared from countries where it was once strongly established – for example, in China, Indo-China and Tibet.

Today, Buddhism is found in Sri Lanka (where 67% of the population are Buddhists). Buddhism is also found in Burma, Thailand, Cambodia, Laos, Vietnam, Japan, Mongolia, Korea, Formosa, some parts of China, Tibet, India, and Pakistan, and even in the Soviet Union. It is also attracting an increasing following in Europe and the United States. There are over 500 million Buddhists throughout the world.

The Buddhist shrines shown on the map are called by different names – such as stupa, dagoba, pagoda and chorten. These shrines show the variations that can be found in Buddhist architecture.

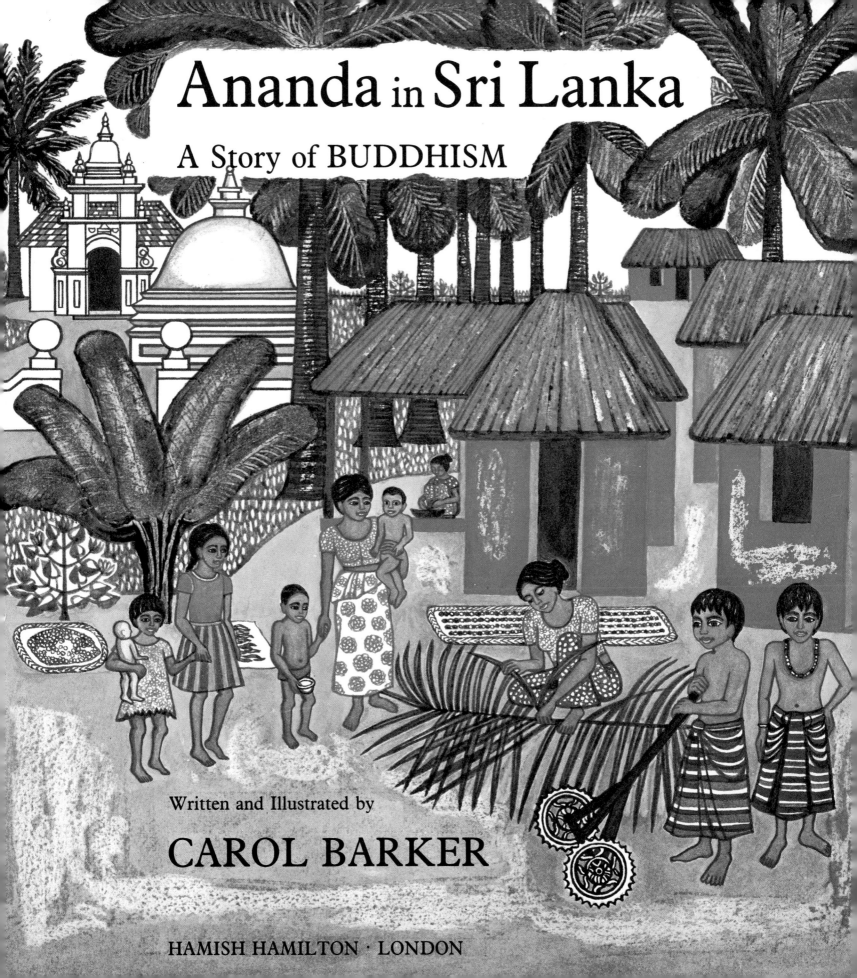

Ananda in Sri Lanka

A Story of BUDDHISM

Written and Illustrated by

CAROL BARKER

HAMISH HAMILTON · LONDON

To Poson

Preface by UNICEF

The springhead of all human cultures is religion: the body of teaching, beliefs, practices and moral principles which establishes the tone and framework for people's relationships with themselves, their communities and their environment, and also provides a meaning for their existence. Singing, dancing, drama, painting and most other forms of artistic expression originated in religion and the feelings they evoke are touched and coloured by religious traditions.

Without an appreciation of this ancient and pervasive element, it is not possible to relate sensitively to other people especially to people in far-away places whose manners, languages and customs seem strange to us. Even well-meaning or charitable impulses directed towards helping them to develop and grow to their full human potential are often found to be counterproductive without such empathy – the ability to put ourselves in the place of others, to feel as they do.

There is a simple English word which has a meaning which possibly has no precise equivalent in any other European language. It is the common word 'kind'. To 'be kind' means to treat like kin. This is what Carol Barker has tried to do in her gentle story of Buddhism, *Ananda in Sri Lanka*. She succeeds in communicating the realities of life in a typically poor family by letting them and those who touch their lives speak for themselves so that the essential nuances which give particular meaning to their living conditions emerge from the narrative.

Buddhism has been the strong central thread of Sri Lanka's history through 2,300 years. During that long period, Sri Lanka has been buffeted by many invasions of different religious forms and political ideas. But, despite benign neglect, as well as some deliberate efforts to suppress the indigenous culture, the teachings of the Buddha have persisted among the majority of the people, particularly in the poor rural communities. The Buddha's values of compassion and tolerance prevail so that other religions followed by minority groups co-exist peacefully with the religion of 80 per cent of the people.

That is why most visitors who have lived among the people long enough to get to know something of their nature and life-ways become devotees of the country. And that is why, materially poor as the people are, Sri Lanka is a rich country.

Tarzie Vittachi
UNICEF, New York

Sri Lanka is a tropical island set in the Indian Ocean. In ancient times, it was known by several names. People in India called it 'The Isle of Gems'; to the merchants of Arabia it was 'The Isle of Delight'; and to the people of Sri Lanka themselves, it was *Lanka dipa*, 'The Resplendent Isle'.

The island lies off the southern tip of India. But although India is so close, and has always had great influence on Sri Lanka (formerly Ceylon), it has kept its independence and its own culture and religion.

Most people in Sri Lanka are Sinhalese, and they speak the Sinhalese language. They are Aryan people who first came from north India: according to legend, Prince Vijaya and his followers arrived on the island in about 500 BC. They settled on the banks of the rivers in the north of Sri Lanka, and began to cultivate rice. So the Sinhalese civilization has been in existence for almost 2,500 years.

The Romans came to Sri Lanka to buy rubies and gems. The Chinese came to trade in silk and textiles. The Arabians came to buy spices such as pepper, cinnamon, cardamom and nutmeg. They travelled to Sri Lanka in trading ships, and when the ships were full, sailed to Persia. From there, the merchants took their goods by camel along overland routes, all the way to Turkey, Greece and Italy.

Buddhism was founded in northern India, and was brought to Sri Lanka during the reign of the Emperor Asoka. It became the main religion of the island, and has remained so for over 2,000 years.

Turuwila is a Buddhist village. It is in a group of six villages built around the edge of the 'tank' (reservoir) from which it gets its name. It is about thirty kilometres south of Anuradhapura – the first sacred city in Sri Lanka. This city became the capital of the first Sinhalese kingdom and the centre of Buddhism.

Life in Turuwila village is centred on the temple, the tank and the paddy-fields (rice fields). Ananda, aged twelve, and his sister Mallika, aged eight, live with their family in Turuwila. Ananda says, 'Today is Sunday. It is also Poya day, which means Full-moon day. This day is the most important in the month for Buddhists. Every Sunday morning, the chief *bhikkhu* (monk) at our temple takes the village children for lessons about Buddhism at the School of *Dharma*. Mallika and I bring lotus flowers and incense to the shrine of the Lord Buddha. We kneel to him in front of the shrine. Then we Buddhists always say the *Tisarana* (the Three Jewels). We recite it in the sacred language of Pali.

Buddham saranam gacchami   I take the Buddha as my refuge
Dhamman saranam gacchami   I take the Dharma as my refuge
Sangham saranam gacchami   I take the Sangha as my refuge

The Buddha was the founder of Buddhism; the Dharma is the Teaching that he gave; and the Sangha is the monastery, the group of monks who follow, and also spread, his Teaching. These three things are very important in the Buddhist religion, and this is why they are called the Three Jewels.'

The chief bhikkhu tells the children about the life of Buddha.

'A long time ago, there was a king named Suddhodana. He lived in the town of Kapilavastu in the foothills of the Himalayas in northern India. His wife, Queen Maya, gave birth to a baby son in the year 560 BC. He was named Siddhartha Gautama. Some wise men came to see the baby, and they foretold that he would either become a great world ruler or a great religious teacher, and that he would see 'Four Signs'. The King wanted his son to rule after him, but he was afraid that Siddhartha might become a religious teacher. So he had three palaces built for the prince, and provided him with all the pleasures the court could offer. Siddhartha grew up in a protected world of luxury. He later married Princess Yasodhara, who bore him a son called Rahula.

Then one day, when Siddhartha was twenty-nine years old, he asked Channa his charioteer to take him for a drive to a nearby village. In all, he went four times. The first time, he saw an old man; the second, a sick man; the third, a dead man. Siddhartha was deeply shocked because he had never seen suffering or death before. Then the fourth time, he saw an ascetic, a holy man who had given up everything to follow the religious life. This man looked calm and peaceful, and it was clear he understood why suffering existed. These then were the Four Signs.

Siddhartha decided to follow the example of the ascetic, the holy man. So one night he slipped out of the palace and rode with Channa to the border. There he took off his silken clothes and jewels and changed into the simple saffron robes of a holy man. He cut off all his beautiful black hair. Then, carrying nothing but a begging bowl for food, he set off alone on his great search.

First, Siddhartha went to the famous religious teachers of his day, and learned all they had to teach. But this did not give him the answer, so he tried another way, by making himself suffer hardship and torment. He sat in the scorching midday sun, he slept on thorns, and he starved himself until he was nothing but skin and bone. For six years Siddhartha searched, but still he did not find the answer to his problem. He realised that this was not the way – and so he took a little food. Then he sat down under a great Bo-tree at a place now called Bodh-Gaya. He determined to sit there until he found the answer, or die trying. He passed into the 'great meditation' and gained various kinds of new knowledge. He emerged from this meditation on Poya day in May (*Wesak*) as the fully Enlightened one, the Buddha.

The Buddha then went to the deer park at Sarnath near Benares, where he preached his first sermon on the Dharma (the Teaching) to five ascetics. They became the first Buddhist monks. The Buddha gathered more followers and monks, and founded the Sangha, the first monastery.

Then for the next forty-five years he spent his life travelling and teaching people. At the age of eighty, he died in Kushinagara. After his death his followers, the bhikkhus, dispersed and went to other parts of India to spread the Dharma to the people.'

Ananda says, 'It is not far from the temple to our house. We walk along the *bund* (bank) surrounding the tank. The tank is like a beautiful lake, with pink and white lotus flowers growing at the far end. On one side there are coconut trees and paddy-fields; and on the other, a thick forest where wild elephants live.

My favourite place to play with my friends is the bund, especially during the windy season in May when we fly paper kites. Sometimes, the strings break and the kites go sailing away over the forest.

My teacher at school has told us about the history of tanks in Sri Lanka. He says that many of the big tanks were built by the first Sinhalese kings more than 2,000 years ago! Our tank at Turuwila was probably built by King Sena I in the ninth century AD, so even that is more than 1,000 years old. Tanks are needed in this area because it is one of the dry parts of the island. The farmers use the water to irrigate their paddy-fields. Without it, they could only grow one crop a year after the north-east monsoon. Now they can grow two. My father is a farmer, and so are the other people in our village. Many of them are related to each other. I have many uncles and cousins living here, and we all help each other working in the fields.

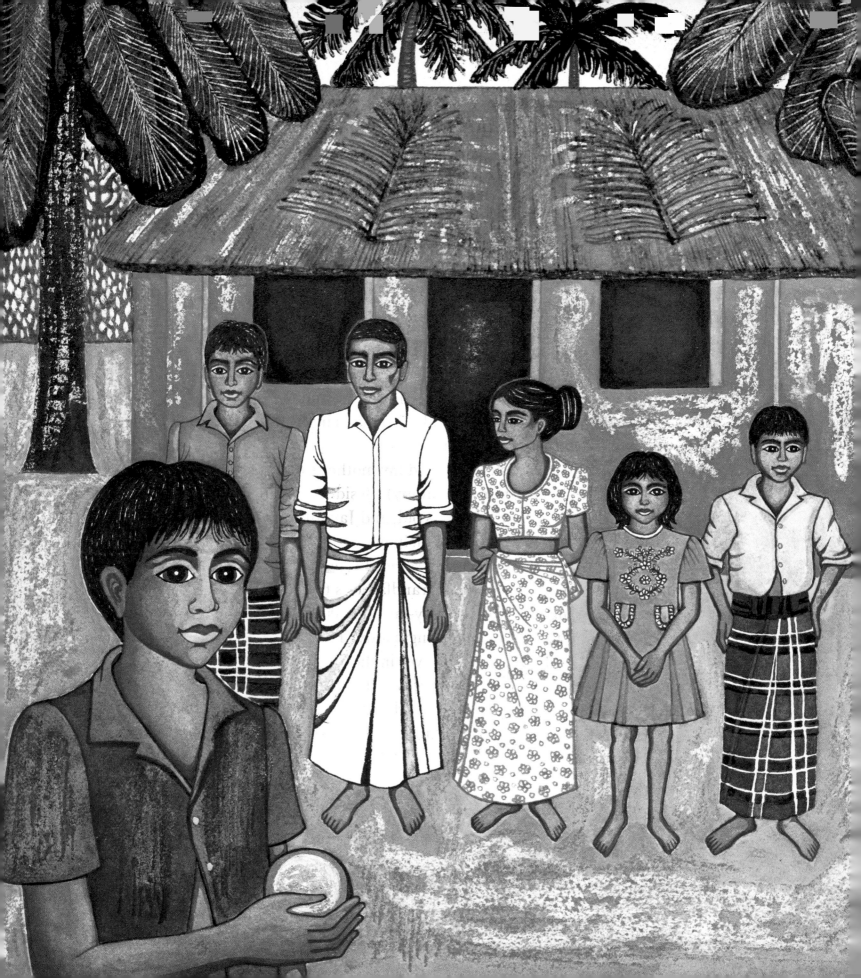

'Our house is on the right-hand side of the tank and the bund. It is surrounded by coconut trees and some banana trees, and lies a short distance away from the other houses in the village. It is made of mud and wattle, and thatched with straw and *cadjan* (coconut palm leaves). Nearly all the houses in the village are made like this. Our house was built by my grandfather.

My father's name is Wijesundara, and my mother's name is Anulawathi. I call them Tatta (Daddy) and Amma (Mummy). Besides my sister Mallika, I have two brothers – Sunil, who is eighteen years old, and Jayatilake, who is fifteen years old. My brothers have left school and they help my father on the farm. Mallika and I still go to school, so we help in the fields on some afternoons and holidays.'

Tatta says, 'From my father's and grandfather's time, my family has grown paddy, so I was brought up to do paddy-farming like my forefathers. I have one hectare of land near the tank for growing paddy. This land belongs to me. I also do *chena* farming on another half hectare over in the forest. This land belongs to the government. Here we clear the small trees and bushes, and plant seedlings which will grow into maize and vegetables. Nearly all our own vegetables are grown on the chena. But growing paddy is our main work. Rice is our staple food, and we usually sell some to buy the things we need.'

Ananda says, 'My mother gets up first in the family, at about 4.30 in the morning. She goes to the nearby well to wash, and to fetch water. She carries the water in a *kalaya* (pottery jar) and a bucket. Then she brings sticks of wood and makes a fire with them in the *lipa* (fireplace) in the kitchen. She puts on a kettle to make tea. At about 5.15, she wakes up my sister Mallika. Mallika sweeps the floor with a broom inside the house and round the outside until it all looks beautifully clean.

'Meanwhile, my mother prepares *rotis* and *sambal* for breakfast. Rotis are like thick pancakes made with flour and water, some grated coconut, and a little sugar. Sambal is made from grated coconut mixed with chilli powder. It tastes very spicy.

At about six o'clock, my mother wakes my father, my two brothers and me. I go to the well to wash, and brush my teeth, then get dressed in my school clothes. By now, Mallika has also washed and changed into her pink school dress. We have breakfast together before the rest of the family. Then we collect our school books and pens and walk to school. We arrive in time to play with our friends before school starts at 7.30.

Amma, my mother, says, "Each morning, after we have all finished eating breakfast and drinking plain tea, my son Jayatilake and I milk the cows. We have three cows and two calves. We have finished milking by 8 o'clock, and then it is time for my husband and sons to go to the paddy-fields. It is harvest time now, and they are working very hard to bring in the ripe paddy and stack it by the threshing ground.

During the morning I prepare lunch for the family. First I put some rice in a large pot to cook on the fire. Then I make two kinds of vegetable curry. After a couple of hours the food is ready. I spoon the rice into a large metal basin and pour the curries into two dishes.

Then I put the dishes and some plates on top of the basin and wrap everything in a large cotton cloth. I place the whole bundle on my head and, balancing it very carefully, walk barefoot along the narrow bunds edging the paddy-fields. After a kilometre or so, I reach the threshing ground where my husband and sons are working. I put the bundle on the ground and spread out the cloth, with the rice bowl in the centre. Then I serve the food for my husband and sons, although I eat only after they have finished. This is the custom in Sri Lanka. After resting for about half an hour, work starts again. I stay with my husband and sons and we work together until around 5 o'clock.'

Ananda's father says, 'In Sri Lanka, there are two seasons a year for growing paddy. The first is the Yala season, from March to September; the second, and the most important, is the Maha season, from October to January. In the Yala season this year, we farmers decided to cultivate all our land. Between us, there are two hundred farmers living here in Turuwila, and we have about 170 hectares of land.

Growing paddy successfully depends on a flow of water from the tank. The water goes along irrigation channels into the paddy-fields. Two sluice gates control exactly how much water is let into the fields so that they do not become too wet or too dry. To grow paddy, the ground is first ploughed by teams of water buffaloes. In May, the paddy seed is sown. When the plants have grown about 15 centimetres tall, the fields are flooded with water. The water continues to flow on and off until the beginning of August.

By August, the paddy is ripe and the water from the tank is shut off so that the fields can dry out in time for the harvest. Now it is harvest time and everyone in the family helps. First the paddy has to be cut. This is usually done by women, working in groups of six to ten. My wife's sisters come to help. They all move slowly forward in a line, cutting the paddy with their sickles. When the paddy has been reaped, it is left for two days to dry in the fields. Then the men collect it into large bundles. This is heavy work. Sunil, my eldest son, helps me carry the bundles of paddy to the bullock cart. Then we take them to the threshing ground.

'The paddy is unloaded and heaped into stacks around the threshing ground. The next evening, if the weather is dry, the paddy is threshed. This is done with a team of water buffaloes, which are trained to walk round and round the threshing ground so that their hooves separate the grains of rice from the stalks. Water buffaloes do not like working in the heat of the day, so they start threshing at dusk, and continue by lamplight through the night. It takes them two nights to thresh one hectare's worth of paddy. Jayatilake usually works with the buffaloes and Ananda helps when he can.

After threshing, the grains of rice are collected and put into sacks. Some are sold

straightaway to grain merchants, while the rest are taken to our house to be stored until needed.' Ananda says, 'After the harvest, my mother cooks some *kiri-bath* (rice cooked in milk) with a little of the newly harvested rice. We take this to the temple and give some to the bhikkhu. We also offer some kiri-bath to the Lord Buddha at the shrine. We give him flowers, too. We thank the Lord Buddha for giving us a successful harvest, and for protecting our families. We also pray to the two gods, Lord Vishnu and Gana-Devi, the guardians of Buddhism at the temple.'

'The chief monk has told us the story of how Buddhism was brought to Sri Lanka,' says Ananda. 'This is what he said. "The great Emperor Asoka of India was a devoted Buddhist and he decided to send his son, Mahinda, to Sri Lanka to spread the Dharma, the Buddha's Teaching. Mahinda was a Buddhist monk who, it is said, descended from the sky with six other monks on to the rock on the top of the mountain at Mihintale in the year 242 BC. On Poya day in June of that year, King Devanampiya Tissa was hunting in the forests around Mihintale mountain.

Suddenly, he noticed a deer grazing in the distance. The deer looked up and, seeing the King, ran off in the direction of Mahinda. The King followed the deer, but it disappeared like magic. Then the King heard his name being called three times, 'Tissa! Tissa! Tissa!'. He was astonished that someone was addressing him by his first name because at that time no-one was allowed to do this. He looked about, and saw Mahinda with the other monks standing under a mango tree. 'Who are you?' he asked. 'And how did you get here?'

Mahinda replied, 'Maharaja, Great King, we are followers of the Lord Buddha, and we have come from India to give you the message of the Buddha's Teaching.' And Mahinda preached a sermon on the Dharma there and then.

King Tissa listened, and he and his followers believed what Mahinda said. They agreed to follow the Teaching of Lord Buddha, and soon everyone else in Sri Lanka decided to follow the new religion of the King. They decided to give up worshipping the sun and the trees, and the spirits and cobras, and they became converted to Buddhism. King Tissa then built many temples and *dagobas* (sacred domes) in Anuradhapura, and a beautiful temple and dagoba at the top of Mihintale mountain. These are still here today and remain two of the most sacred places in Sri Lanka. During the festival of *Poson* at the end of June, thousands of people travel from all over the island to worship at the temples there and to celebrate the coming of Buddhism to Sri Lanka." '

Ananda says, 'Mallika and I go to Turuwila primary school. It starts at 7.30 a.m. with morning assembly. We sing songs in honour of the Lord Buddha in front of our little temple in the school grounds. Then classes start at 7.45. Mallika is in Grade 3 and I am in Grade 5. We have lessons every morning until 1.30, with one break when we play with our friends.

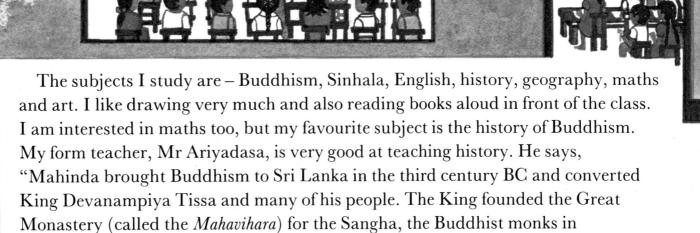

The subjects I study are – Buddhism, Sinhala, English, history, geography, maths and art. I like drawing very much and also reading books aloud in front of the class. I am interested in maths too, but my favourite subject is the history of Buddhism. My form teacher, Mr Ariyadasa, is very good at teaching history. He says, "Mahinda brought Buddhism to Sri Lanka in the third century BC and converted King Devanampiya Tissa and many of his people. The King founded the Great Monastery (called the *Mahavihara*) for the Sangha, the Buddhist monks in Anuradhapura. From here, the monks preached to the people. This became the centre of the teaching of the 'Elders', the *Theravada* School of Buddhism in Sri Lanka.

Soon after this, the King invited Mahinda's sister, Sanghamitta, to start an Order for nuns. She came from north India, bringing with her a branch of the sacred Bo-tree from Bodh-Gaya. This was planted in Anuradhapura and grew into a huge pipal tree, which can still be seen today. It is a very sacred tree, and is much revered by the people.

King Devanampiya Tissa was the first king of many to build great temples and dagobas in Sri Lanka. After him, King Dutugemunu built four other important dagobas, including the *Ruvanvalisaya*, which is the biggest and most beautiful dagoba on the island. Inside, there is a huge chamber in which are kept jewels and sacred relics. So, for many hundreds of years, the kings of Sri Lanka played an important part in the development of the Sangha.

In 80 BC, a very important event took place. A council meeting was held in a cave temple in Matale, and for the first time the Teaching of the Buddha was written down. Until then, the Teaching had only been passed on by word of mouth. Sri Lanka became the main centre in the world of the Theravada School of Buddhism, and scholar monks from China and other countries came to copy the scriptures."

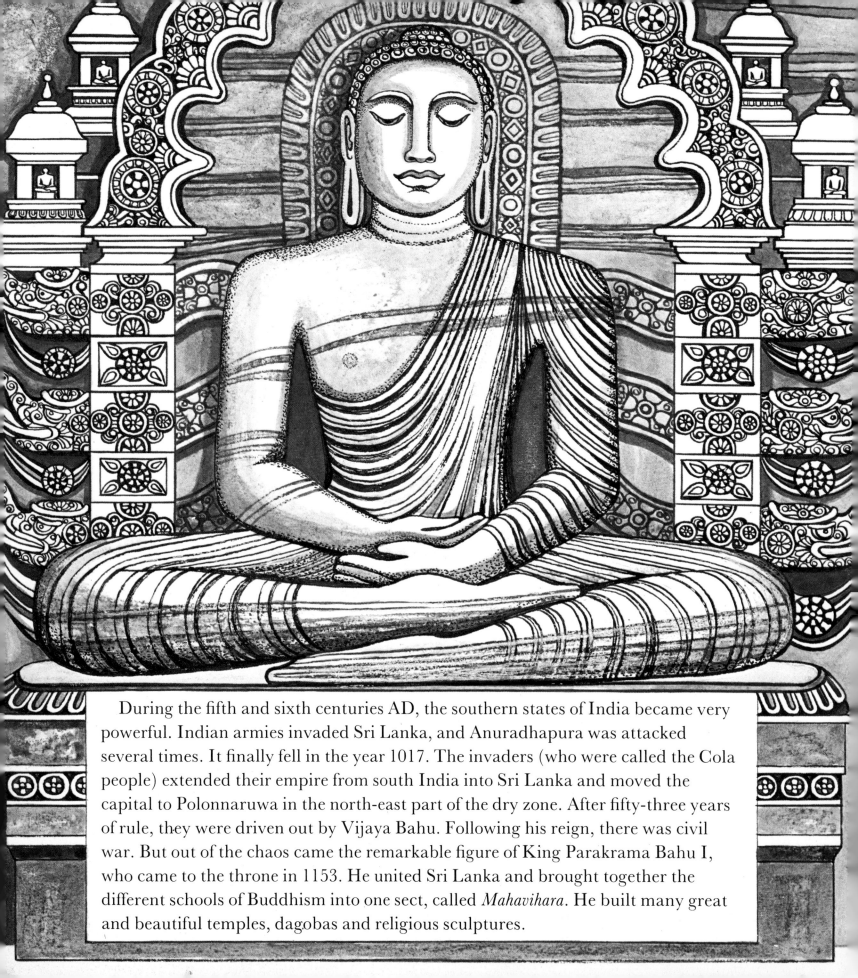

During the fifth and sixth centuries AD, the southern states of India became very powerful. Indian armies invaded Sri Lanka, and Anuradhapura was attacked several times. It finally fell in the year 1017. The invaders (who were called the Cola people) extended their empire from south India into Sri Lanka and moved the capital to Polonnaruwa in the north-east part of the dry zone. After fifty-three years of rule, they were driven out by Vijaya Bahu. Following his reign, there was civil war. But out of the chaos came the remarkable figure of King Parakrama Bahu I, who came to the throne in 1153. He united Sri Lanka and brought together the different schools of Buddhism into one sect, called *Mahavihara*. He built many great and beautiful temples, dagobas and religious sculptures.

The most magnificent of these is the *Gal Vihara*, the rock temple with three figures cut out of the rock; the *samadhi* Buddha seated in meditation, the standing figure (thought to be Ananda, the Buddha's favourite disciple), and the reclining Buddha. King Parakrama Bahu I ruled until 1186 and was the last great Sinhalese king. During his reign, the kingdom of Polonnaruwa reached the height of its power. His successor ruled for only ten years. Then Polonnaruwa too had to be abandoned because of more invasions from India. The third and last kingdom in Sri Lanka was in Kandy, high up in the mountains.

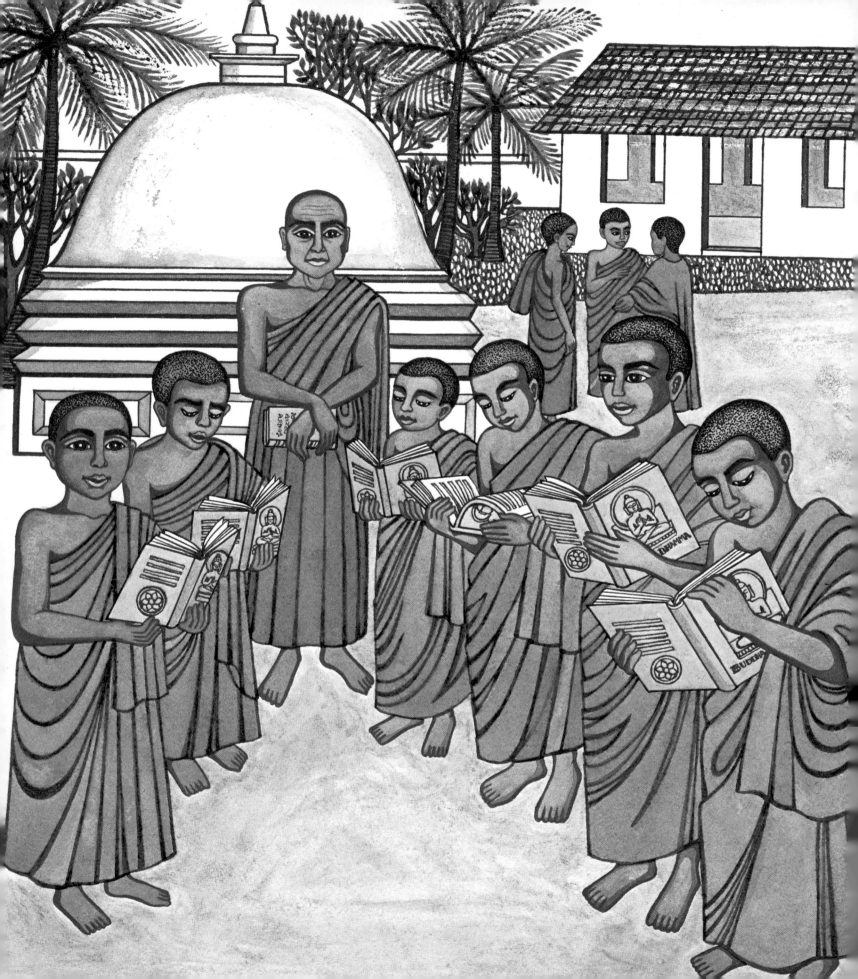

The temple at Turuwila is also the chief temple for the five other villages around the tank. The chief monk says, 'People in this village look up to me. If they need help or advice, they come to me first. They also ask for a blessing before they are married, before they start on a long journey, or for a new house. I, with other monks, perform religious ceremonies at funerals and on special festival days like *Wesak* and *Poson*. I also visit the houses of the sick, and chant *Pirith* (sacred Pali verses) to help them in their suffering. I take Dharma School on Sunday mornings and, on Sunday evenings, I preach a sermon and take prayers and meditation.

I am also the head of the *Pirivena*, the monks' training school. It takes a long time to become a monk and it needs a long, special training. A boy's parents who wish their son to become a monk bring him to me at the age of six or seven. They leave him at the monastery to study with several other boys and novice monks. He takes lessons in Pali and Sanskrit, as well as in maths, history, Sinhala and English. He learns many Pali verses by heart, and recites them to me. After five years, when the boy is eleven or twelve, the parents are invited back to the temple. Once again, they are asked if they want their child to become a monk. If the answer is yes, and I feel that the boy is clever enough and suited to the life, then a special ceremony takes place. First the boy's head is shaved and he has a bath. Then he is given the saffron yellow robes of a monk to dress in, and a wooden bowl to carry food in. Finally, he is given an umbrella. All these things are provided by his parents. Now he is a young monk and is called *Samanera bhikkhu*.

The boy continues his studies with one tutor monk. He has to obey strict rules and keep his vows to give up all worldly goods and pleasures. When he is twenty, there is the Ordination Ceremony when he becomes a monk, an *Upasampada bhikkhu*. Now he can choose to stay here in Turuwila, or go to another temple. He can give his own sermons and preach the Dharma to the people in villages or in towns. It is his own choice. However, it is not only boys who become monks. Men can also become monks later in life, if they want to renounce the world and become bhikkhus.

The chief monk says. 'The most important Buddhist festival of the year is *Wesak*. This festival celebrates the Birth, the Enlightenment, and the Death of the Buddha. It takes place on Poya day in May.'

Ananda says, 'People bring decorations for the temple and the Bo-tree, and they hang coloured Wesak lanterns all over the temple gardens. I go with all the other children from the village to form a procession. We carry lanterns, decorations, burning torches and dishes of flowers. The procession starts at 7 p.m., and later on our parents join in. We walk around the temple and gardens three or four times. Then we stop at the shrine and put our offerings of flowers on the altar of Lord Buddha. The chief monk gives a Dharma sermon and the monks chant *Pirith*. Then it is time to go home. Buddhists all over Sri Lanka celebrate Wesak like this.'